Dinah!

a cat
adventure

Story and pictures by KAE NISHIMURA

CLARION BOOKS · NEW YORK

Clarion Books
a Houghton Mifflin Company imprint
215 Park Avenue South, New York, NY 10003
Copyright © 2004 by Kae Nishimura

The illustrations were executed in watercolor.
The text was set in 18-point Frutiger Condensed.

www.houghtonmifflinbooks.com

Printed in Singapore

Library of Congress Cataloging-in-Publication Data
Nishimura, Kae.
Dinah! / by Kae Nishimura.
p. cm.
Summary: Dinah, an overfed, pampered housecat,
falls out a window and into an unknown world,
where she is mistaken for a raccoon, a watermelon,
and a tiger before rediscovering her true identity.
ISBN 0-618-33612-5
[1. Cats—Fiction. 2. Identity—Fiction. 3. Humorous stories.]
I. Title.
PZ7.N639Di 2004
[E]—dc22
2003011246

TWP   10 9 8 7 6 5 4 3 2 1

For Pat Cummings and Guy Billout

A family got a tiny cat. They named her Dinah, and they loved her very much.

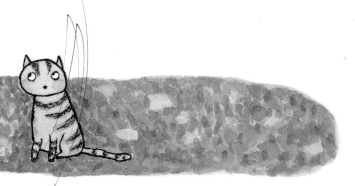

Every day at breakfast, when no one else was around,
Father would give Dinah a piece of egg and say, "Here,
princess. It's our secret."

When Mother got ready to leave for work, she made sure
no one was looking, and then she gave Dinah some milk.
"Here, baby," she would say. "It's our secret."

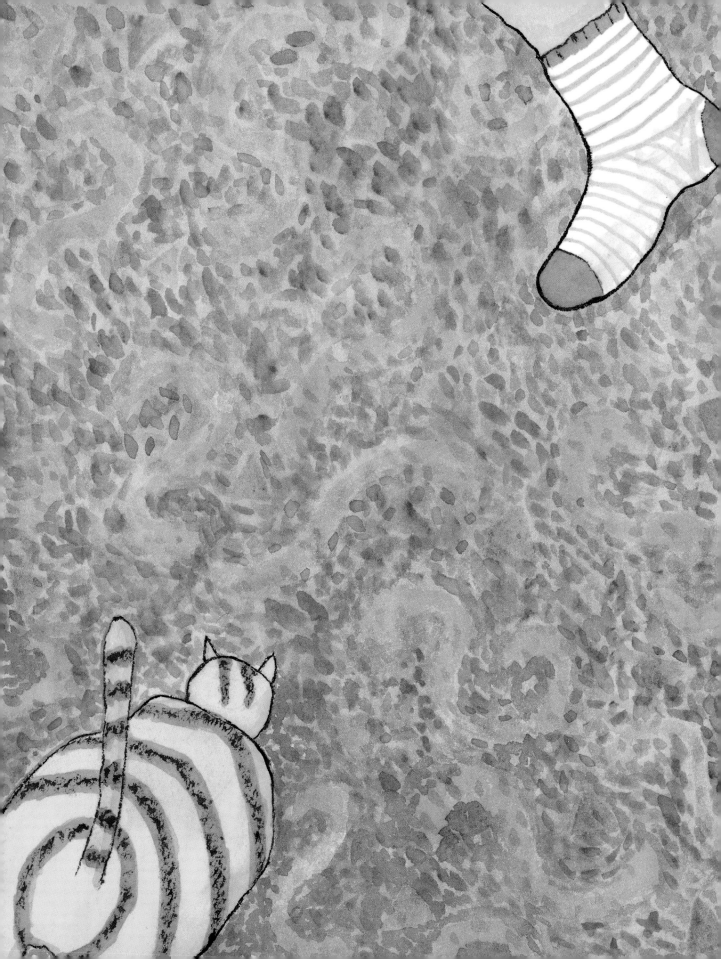

Every day, when they were alone, Boy shared his
after-school cookie with Dinah, saying, "Here, friend.
It's our secret."

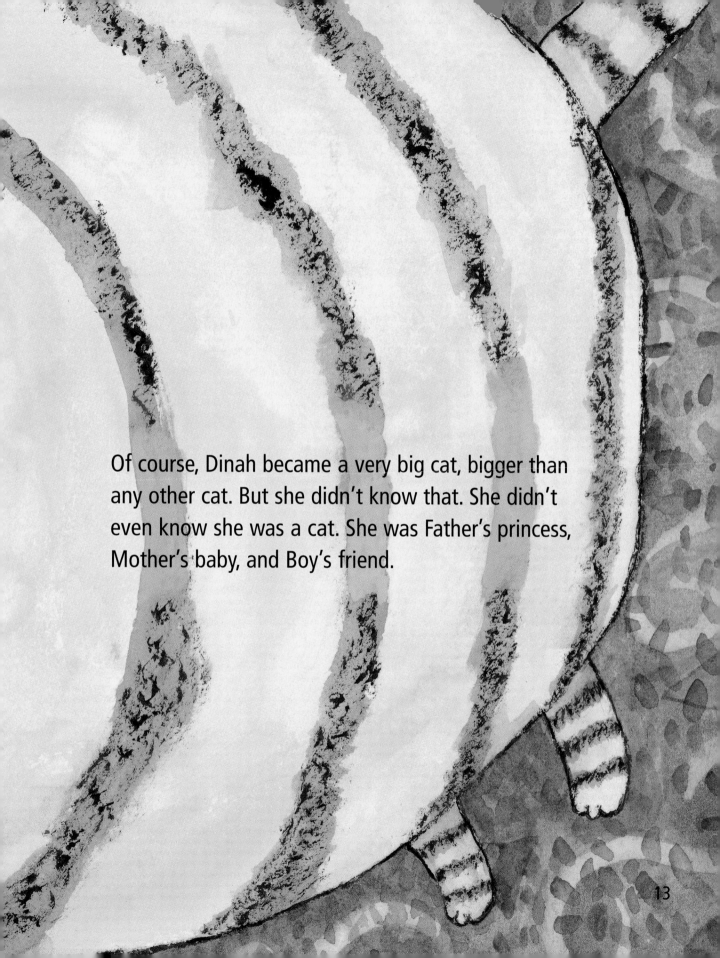

Of course, Dinah became a very big cat, bigger than any other cat. But she didn't know that. She didn't even know she was a cat. She was Father's princess, Mother's baby, and Boy's friend.

Since the day she came to the family's home, Dinah had never been outdoors. Sometimes she wondered what was on the other side of the window. One day when she tried to see out, the window was open. And out she fell!

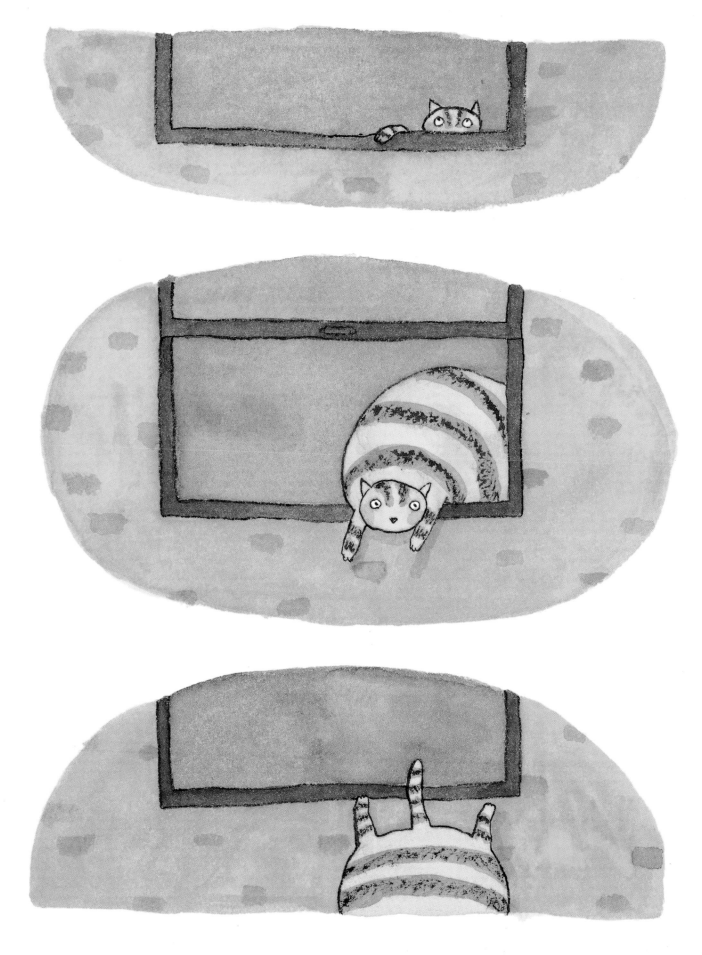

She rolled from rooftop to rooftop, all the way down to the ground.

18

When Dinah opened her eyes, she had no idea where she was.
The first thing she saw was an old lady. "What are you doing
here, raccoon?" the old lady asked.

"I am not Raccoon," said Dinah. "I am Princess Baby Friend.
I am looking for my home."

The old lady said, "Raccoons are not princesses. Raccoons live
in the forest." She pointed down the road.

Dinah started walking.

19

After a while, Dinah stopped to
rest under a fruit vendor's wagon.
When the vendor noticed her, he
said, "What's this? A runaway
watermelon?"

"I am not Watermelon,"
Dinah answered. "I am
Baby Friend."

20

The vendor looked at Dinah carefully. "You are not a baby, you are a grown-up," he said. "A grown-up watermelon. And now you are for sale."

Many people stopped to buy watermelon, but no one bought Dinah. "That watermelon is too hairy," they said.

Soon only Dinah was left. The vendor wheeled his wagon away, leaving her on the street.

A big flock of sheep came toward Dinah, and suddenly she was in the middle of them. As she tried to find a way out, the shepherd poked her with his stick. "You aren't like the others!" he shouted. "What kind of sheep are you?"

"I am not Sheep," Dinah answered. "I am Friend."
"You are not *my* friend," said the shepherd. "You are a fat little tiger, and you'll try to eat my precious sheep. Get out of here!"
Dinah ran.

23

It was starting to get dark. Dinah felt lonely and lost. A dog came walking along the street. "Where is my house?" Dinah asked him.

"Your house?" the dog replied. "Who are you?"

"I am . . ." Dinah hesitated. She wasn't sure anymore. "Who do you think I am?"

"You're asking *me* who you are?" The dog studied Dinah. "Well, let me see. You look very different from the cats I know, but you are a cat."

"A cat?" Dinah repeated. Could that be right?

But the dog added, "And dogs always attack cats!" He growled and jumped at Dinah.

As Dinah escaped, she was thinking hard.

"I thought I was Princess. And Baby. And Friend. But the old lady said I was a raccoon living in the forest. The fruit vendor said I was a watermelon to be sold. Or I might be a tiger that eats precious sheep. And the dog says I am a cat, and he attacked me. Who am I?"

Just then, Dinah heard voices.

She knew those voices. It was Father, Mother, and Boy.

"Dinah!" called Father.

"Dinah!" called Mother.

"Dinah!" called Boy.

And now she knew who she was! "Yes, I am Dinah," she said. "That is my name." She ran to meet them.

"We were so worried about you," they said, and they hugged her and carried her home.